The Whippersnapper

Taggart Neher

PAGE PUBLISHING, INC.
Conneaut Lake, PA

First originally published by Page Publishing 2021

ISBN 978-1-6624-5580-3 (hc)
ISBN 978-1-6624-5581-0 (digital)

Printed in the United States of America

This book is dedicated to my three daughters Kaitlin, Ella, and Sarah. I love you with all my heart, mind, and soul for infinity.

One evening, while staying at Grandpa and Grandma's house, three little sisters were preparing for bed. They'd been having fun all day with Grandma. They knew she was busy in the kitchen and decided to go see what Grandpa was doing. He was sitting in his favorite chair, in the living room, reading a book. The three sisters decided to ask him to tell them a story, so they wouldn't have to go straight to bed. Grandpa agreed to tell them a story, and this is what happened next…

Grandpa started the story by saying, "Once upon a time, there was a whippersnapper that lived deep in the Black Forest in a hidden village named Froda Stattle Fiddle Faddle Ring Ding Doo."

Immediately, the three sisters interrupted Grandpa and exclaimed, "Oh, come on, Grandpa; tell us a real story! There is no such thing as the Black Forest and a village named Froda Stattle…whatever you said."

Grandpa replied, "You've never heard of the Black Forest?"

The girls said, "No, that sounds creepy, and you're just trying to scare us, but it's not going to work this time, Grandpa."

Grandpa replied, "Well, you three are smart little girls with your devices and all that fancy technology stuff. Why don't you just search on the internet for the Black Forest and tell me whether it's real or not?"

The girls immediately agreed to do that as they giggled among each other because they just knew they had caught Grandpa in a fib. To their amazement though, when they searched online for the Black Forest, they found it. It was a forest in Germany. The three sisters were surprised it was a real place, so they looked at Grandpa and said, "Okay, Grandpa, tell us more of the story, but seriously Froda Staddle…whatever the name of that hidden village was can't be real."

Grandpa said, "Well, yes, it is…in fact it's not too far from the village of Isa Bella Oten Boten Coomalatta Compatary Esaburro Lotta Fotta Copenhagen Stupor."

The girls instantly erupted again with disbelief and said, "Okay, Grandpa, now we know your making this up because there is no such place called that!"

Grandpa again told them, "If you don't believe me, then use those fancy devices of yours and search for a town called Copenhagen. I bet you will find it north of Germany and the Black Forest."

Again, the girls went to search for the place online, but this time, they weren't as confident about catching Grandpa in a fib, since last time he was actually right. Sure enough, they found a place called Copenhagen, and yes, it was north of Germany and the Black Forest. The girls started to think that just maybe Grandpa was telling them a real story.

"Okay, Grandpa, tell us more." This time the girls said it with curiosity rather than laughter and disbelief of Grandpa.

So Grandpa continued his story about the whippersnapper, who lived deep in the Black Forest, in a hidden village named Froda Stattle Fiddle Faddle Ring Ding Doo, not too far from the village of Isa Bella Oten Boten Coomalatta Compatary Esaburro Lotta Fotta Copenhagen Stupor.

"The whippersnapper has three toes but no arms and no legs," Grandpa said.

All three little girls burst into laughter and interrupted Grandpa once again. "That's impossible, Grandpa! You can't have three toes with no legs. Now we know you are just trying to trick us. The little girls laughed and rolled on the floor in front of Grandpa. They just knew he was fibbing now."

Grandpa replied to his granddaughters, "Well, you girls won't even let me tell the story. I'll just go back to reading my book."

He reached for his book, but before he could pick it up, the girls pleaded, "No, Grandpa, tell us the rest of the story. We believe you, but some of it probably isn't true." They giggled and hoped Grandpa would continue to tell them the rest of the story.

Grandpa said, "Okay." After all, he knew the girls were having fun. They were laughing and giggling. Grandpa was having fun too. He enjoyed hearing them laugh and giggle. He was happy just to be with them.

"Alright, so one morning the whippersnapper woke up and drove his car to work." Grandpa continued, "The whippersnapper worked at a coffee shop in the village, but this morning, when he arrived at the coffee shop, it was so busy that there was nowhere to park. The only place he could find to park his car was in a no parking zone. He didn't want to be late for work, so he parked there. After work, he saw a tow truck was hooked up to his car and was towing it away. The whippersnapper was frustrated, but he knew he had two more vehicles at home he could use. The next morning, he took his truck to work. The same thing happened. It was so busy he had to park in the no parking zone again. After work, the same tow truck had hooked up to his truck and towed it away, also. That's two times this has happened now. He still wasn't worried because he had another vehicle at home. The third morning, he drove his van to work. Yup, it was so busy he had to park in the no parking zone, and yes, again after work, he saw the tow truck towing his van away. The whippersnapper was very upset. 'That makes three toes I have now!'" he whimpered.

Grandpa looked at his granddaughters with a twinkle in his eyes and said, "See, I told you the whippersnapper has three toes but no arms and no legs."

The girls instantly burst into laughter. "Oh, my goodness, Grandpa, that's too funny! Seriously, Grandpa, you tricked us." They giggled and giggled and tears of laughter began running down their faces. The girls said, "Keep going, Grandpa, and tell us more. What happens next?"

Grandpa said, "I didn't trick you. I told you the whippersnapper had three toes but no arms and no legs. How is that tricking you?"

The oldest sister spoke up first and said, "You made us believe the whippersnapper had no arms and no legs but had three toes...*three toes*, like the ones you can put paint on to make them pretty."

The second oldest sister said, "Yes, Grandpa, that's what I thought you meant...not three tows as in having your car towed away."

Then the youngest sister a bit confused said, "Well, Grandpa, what is it? What's the truth about the whippersnapper? Does he have three toes or not?"

Grandpa replied, "Well, you girls keep interrupting me, and I can't tell the story. I'll just go back to reading my book."

The youngest little girl bounced up off the floor and ran and grabbed grandpa's book before he could reach it. "No, Grandpa, no, please tell us more of the story."

"Please, Grandpa!" The older sisters chimed in, "Please, Grandpa, tell us more!"

It was starting to get late he thought. The girls were up past their bedtime already. Plus, Grandpa was thinking about that yummy food that Grandma had made earlier for dinner. He wanted to sneak into the kitchen and get some of the leftovers that Grandma had put away in the refrigerator. He thought about it for a few moments and then he decided to tell the girls…

"Well, it's already eleventy-seven past your bedtime. Your mommy said to make sure you were in bed every night close to bedtime."

The oldest sister spoke up and said, "Grandpa, eleventy-seven is not a real number."

Grandpa replied, "Yes, it is."

The second oldest said, "No, Grandpa, it's not a real number. Besides, you let us stay up past our bedtime a lot, and I want to hear the rest of the story before we go to bed."

The youngest sister said, "Listen, sissies, we keep telling Grandpa he's wrong, and we don't listen to him. Maybe eleventy-seven is a real number. Is it grandpa?"

Grandpa said, "If you count by tens, what comes after twenty?"

The oldest sister said, "Thirty."

Grandpa said, "What comes after thirty?"

All three girls screamed, "Forty!"

Grandpa said, "Keep counting by tens as high as you can."

So they counted, "Twenty, thirty, forty, fifty, sixty, seventy, eighty, ninety…"

Then the second oldest sister shouted out, "I get it! I know what Grandpa means! If ninety equals 90, then eleventy must be 110. Then you add seven and it makes 117. See, sissies, eleventy-seven equals 117."

The youngest sister was still confused, but the oldest sister said, "You're right! That's what Grandpa means. It's 117 minutes past our bedtime."

Suddenly, the room went quiet. Nobody wanted to say a word after they all realized they were way, way, way passed their bedtime. You could hear a pin drop and hit the floor it was so quiet.

Then, like the sun beaming through the clouds on a cold rainy day, Grandma came into the living room with fresh baked cookies and a delicious looking fruit salad.

"Is anyone ready for a late-night snack?" she said.

"*Me! Me! Me!*" the girls replied with excitement.

Meanwhile, Grandpa knew this could be the perfect chance to sneak away and head to the kitchen to make him a tasty little snack from the leftovers in the refrigerator. He quietly stood up and snuck away while the girls were distracted with all the yummy cookies, fruit, and Grandma's glorious presence.

While Grandma and the girls snacked on the fruit salad and freshly baked cookies, they made their plans for the next day.

The youngest girl said, "Grandma, can we make those yummy pancakes again for breakfast?"

"Of course, we can," Grandma said.

All the girls shouted, "*Yay!*"

"Grandma, can we go pick more blueberries tomorrow? Can we make more homemade bread, and can we plant more stuff in the garden?" said the oldest sister.

"Yes, we will do that and much more tomorrow," Grandma said.

"Grandma, can we go play at the park tomorrow? Can we feed the ducks?" said the youngest sister.

"Yes." Grandma said, "We will do that too."

Meanwhile, Grandpa is trying to be very quiet in the kitchen while he makes a plate of leftovers from dinner.

13

Then, suddenly…grandma hollered…"Grandpa, are you going to finish the story for your granddaughters?"

He replied, "Yes, honey, I'm about to do that after I'm finished making a snack."

Grandma said, "Don't eat everything. Leave some for tomorrows lunch."

Grandpa replied, "Okay, honey." All the while grumbling to himself.

Then, Grandma asked the three little girls, "Have you ever heard the story about the whippersnapper?"

All three girls replied together, "Yes, Grandma, we were just listening to Grandpa tell us the story, but he didn't finish."

"What is a whippersnapper, Grandma?" asked the youngest sister.

She replied, "You are smart little girls. Go grab your devices and search online for what a whippersnapper is."

The girls answered, "Okay, Grandma."

They ran to their devices to search for what it meant. With confidence, they now begin to think that maybe Grandpa was fibbing the whole time. Maybe Grandma knows something they don't. With excitement, they started searching for information.

"I found it!" said the oldest sister. "The dictionary says a whippersnapper is a young or inexperienced person considered to be presumptuous or overconfident."

With her mouth contorted and struggling to repeat such a big word, the youngest sister asked, "Grandma, what does pwe-some-choo-us mean?"

She replied, "Well, it's kind of like when a person offers advice to someone and it's really not needed. Like when I'm baking cookies and Grandpa comes in to tell me that I need to bake the cookies for twenty minutes. That's Grandpa being presumptuous because Grandma already knows how long to bake the cookies."

"Then Grandpa was tricking us with his story about the whippersnapper. It's not a person with no arms, no legs, and three toes. It's just a word from the dictionary. Right, Grandma?" said the second oldest sister.

"Well, it's definitely a person, but whether or not it has no arms, no legs, and three toes, I'm not sure about that. However, I have met a whippersnapper before. Do you girls want to hear about the time I met a whippersnapper?" Grandma asked.

18

"*Yes! Yes! Yes!*" the sisters squealed.

"Well, a long time ago, when I was a young teenager, my parents and I lived in Germany. My father was a doctor, and my mother was a nurse. They worked every day except on Sunday. Back then, there were no buses to ride home after school. You either had to walk home or some of the more fortunate boys and girls would ride home on their bicycles. If you were really lucky, some people had cars, but you rarely saw them in those days, at least not in the smaller villages."

Grandma paused for a moment as she picked up her knitting that she had left out earlier and put it away.

"Anyways, after school, I was walking home, and I decided to stop at the coffee shop to buy a donut. When I walked into the coffee shop, I was greeted by a handsome young man who worked there. He said, 'Welcome to the shop. Please, look around and let me know if I can help you with anything.' I replied by telling him thank you and continued to look throughout the store gazing at all the delicious donuts and other pastries behind the glass counter. I couldn't decide which donut I wanted the most. It's hard to select a donut when there are so many to choose from."

All three girls nodded in an agreement.

"Then the young man spoke up and said, 'That donut with the white powder is called snowball. It costs five cents.' I thought to myself, *I already know that because it says five cents on the price tag, and it also says it's called a snowball.* I didn't want to be rude to the young man, so I didn't reply to him. Then a moment later he said, 'This one over here is a delicious donut. It's seven cents and is called the fudge monster.' Again, the price tag clearly says this, and at this point, he must think I can't read or something. I giggled quietly in my head as to not let him know I was amused."

The girls giggled.

"About a minute later, he said, 'How about this donut over here. It's one of my favorites.' I walked over to the donut he was pointing at. When I looked at the donut, it was called no arms, no legs, with three toes. It was a funny shaped donut. A long oval donut with three tiny smaller donuts connected to the bottom of it. It kind of looked like a person with no arms or legs, but it had three toes."

Right then the oldest sister interrupted Grandma. "Oh, my goodness, I think…I think I know what's going on!"

The other two sisters joined in. "Yes, this must be what Grandpa was talking about!"

But before Grandma could continue the story, Grandpa returned from the kitchen with his late-night leftovers from dinner. "Yes, girls, back in those days, I was young and very confident. Sometimes I was a bit too presumptuous."

The girls laughed, and Grandma smiled. The youngest sister said, "Grandpa, were you that young man at the donut shop, the presumptuous one?"

He replied, "Yes, that was me. That's where I met your grandma for the first time. I owned that coffee shop, and one of my donuts was called no arms, no legs, with three toes."

Grandma then said, "Yes, Grandpa was very confident that day and a little too presumptuous. I told your grandpa, 'I'll buy that donut, you whippersnapper.' He replied back to me by saying what is a whippersnapper?"

The three little girls broke into laughter once again.

Grandma said, "I told your grandpa that day that a whippersnapper has no arms, no legs, and three toes."

Again, the girls laughed and rolled on the floor.

Then, Grandpa asked his granddaughters, "What's green and eats stone?"

The girls immediately asked, "Tell us, Grandpa. What's green and eats stone?"

Grandma interrupted and said, "It's getting late, and we all need to go to bed. That's a story for another day, right, Grandpa?"

Grandpa answered, "I guess it is, Grandma. It's not eleventy-seven past our bedtime anymore. It's way later than that, so let's all go to bed and get a good night sleep."

The three sisters stretched and yawned as they headed for bed, all the while muttering amongst themselves, wondering what in the world is green and eats stone."

As the girls scuttled down the hallway to their bedroom, between yawns, the youngest sister said, "I guess, sissies, we will have to wait for Grandpa to tell us about that story tomorrow night." Sleepily they all agreed.

To be continued…

About the Author

Taggart currently lives in the great state of Texas. He has three children, Kaitlin, Ella, and Sarah. His professional experience includes engineering for the oil and gas industry, a home builder, and is a veteran of the United States Marine Corps. Currently, he focuses most of his time with his family, construction, art, and writing.

CPSIA information can be obtained
at www.ICGtesting.com
Printed in the USA
BVHW091544231121
622342BV00006B/414

9 781662 455803